The Ring of Truth

by

Alan Durant

First published in 2001 in Great Britain by
Barrington Stoke Ltd, Sandeman House, Trunk's Close,
55 High Street, Edinburgh EH1 1SR

This edition published 2004

ISBN 1-842991-91-4

Printed by Polestar Wheatons Ltd

A Note from the Author – Alan Durant

I knew from the age of 14 that I was going to be a writer. My English teacher wasn't so sure. He said my writing was interesting but I never kept to the point. Well, that is the point! To be a writer you have to make any subject your own, turn it into what interests you and say what you need to say. Back then I always wrote about the Crucifixion because that's what interested, no obsessed, me.

I sent my first book to a famous agent. She turned it down because she said it was too unpleasant. But in the end I found someone who liked the book enough to publish it. I grinned for days when they told me. I've written over 40 books now but I still get the same thrill when someone wants to publish my work.

I love thrillers and I loved writing this book. It's the kind of book I would like to read myself – and I hope you enjoy it too. If you don't, feel free to write and say so. Just don't tell me it's too unpleasant or that I haven't kept to the point!

This book is dedicated to my mother, Joy Durant, with a lifetime's love – and more.

Contents

Chapter 1
Discovery

I was going to say it all started when we found the ring. But Fish says it started before that – and he's right (as usual!).

Fish is my best mate. We live in the same street. We go to the same school. We do most things together.

Most days we go to this place we've found on the Common. Fish reckons it's an old air-raid shelter from the Second World War. I like to think it's a prehistoric cave.

"You've got too much imagination," he says.

"Yeah, well, it beats real life," I say.

But Fish won't agree with that. He always looks on the bright side. If I'd been born paralysed from the waist down and had to spend my life in a wheelchair, I'd be right ratty. But not Fish. He just shrugs and says it's the way things are. He hates people making a big thing of it. He has a right go at me sometimes, if he thinks I'm being too protective or trying to give him help when he doesn't need it. His chair is electric anyway so he doesn't need much help.

One time I *do* have to help him is getting into our secret place. There's a step to go down. It was while we were bumping the chair down the step that we discovered the ring. It had got caught in a crack in the step and Fish's back wheel flicked it out.

"Hey, look at that!" I said. I picked it up. It was a large, gold ring with the letter 'T' on it. I showed it to Fish. "It's pretty heavy. I reckon it's made of real gold."

I gave the ring to Fish. "You're right," he said. "Must be worth a bit. We ought to hand it in to the police."

"Mmm," I said. Fish had got me thinking. "Let's not give it in just yet," I said. "There might be a reward." Fish looked at me sort of oddly. He knew it wasn't like me to say something like that. I'm normally a very honest person. I'm always landing myself in trouble, 'cos I can't help telling the truth.

"I need all the money I can get, Fish," I said. "For Darren." Darren was my older brother. He was in rehab trying to kick his drug habit.

Fish nodded. What Darren really needed was something to look forward to, like a holiday. That's what the doctor guy had told Dad, the last time we'd been to visit. The problem was, we were pretty hard up. Dad had given up his job to look after Darren and me after Mum died. That had been over six years ago.

"Let's just wait a few days," I said. "Then we'll hand it in, I promise. OK?"

"OK," Fish agreed.

Little did we know just where that ring would lead us ...

Chapter 2
First Meeting

They found the body a couple of days later. It was hidden in the undergrowth covered in leaves.

Fish and I couldn't go to our secret place on the Common that afternoon. There was yellow tape all around the area. There were police everywhere. They wouldn't tell us what was going on, but we read about it later in the local paper. A man had been shot. The papers said it was a gangland killing, something to do with drugs. Well, there were plenty of drugs round where we lived and didn't I know it. They'd got Darren hooked. I hated drug dealers from the bottom of my heart.

"Well, if he was pushing drugs, I'm glad he's dead," I said.

"You don't mean that," Fish said. "Anyway, the papers might have got it wrong."

That's Fish for you: Mister Reasonable.

The police put out a request for information. There was a notice on the Common asking for anyone who'd seen anything odd or suspicious on the day of the murder to come forward.

Fish said we ought to tell the police about the ring. "It might have something to do with the murder," he said.

I hadn't thought about that. "I don't see how," I said. I didn't want to give the ring up yet. But I felt a bit guilty. "I'll tell you what," I said, "why don't we go down the police station and see what we can find out?"

"Why should they tell *us* anything?" Fish said with a shake of his head.

"We'll just tell them about our den. We won't tell them we found the ring," I said. "We can ask them if they're looking for anything in particular. Offer our help in the search."

"You're crazy, Ros," Fish said, but he agreed to go with me all the same.

I decided that if the police mentioned the ring, then I'd give it to them straight away. But they didn't. In fact they hardly talked to us at all. You could tell from the way they treated us that they thought we were a couple of geeky kids, wasting their time.

Still, we were used to that. Fish has had to put up with that his whole life. It's amazing how many people act like he's stupid just 'cos he's in a wheelchair. As for me, well, I've got spiky, bright pink hair and a nose ring, so I must be a nutter, mustn't I?

I was fuming. As we went back home, I was giving Fish a right ear bashing.

Just as he was telling me to, "Calm down," for about the hundredth time, a big, white car drew up beside the kerb in front of us. I didn't pay it much attention, but as we came alongside, a man's voice called out to us, "Hey, you!"

We stopped and looked over. A pudgy-faced man with a squashed, broken nose like a boxer's was beckoning to us through the open car window. "Over here," he ordered. "I want a word."

I looked at Fish. He looked at me. It was one of those offers you dared not refuse.

"I seen you two down by the Common,

haven't I?" he said.

We nodded.

"So what you been doing down the Old Bill, then, eh? Got something to tell 'em, have you?"

He spoke casual like, as if he wasn't really that interested. But I knew he was. And I recognised the bloke sitting next to him. He was one of the dealers who used to hang about outside our school. We called him Chimp. The moment I saw him, I felt the anger rising.

"I found something," I said. "Near where that bloke was murdered."

"Oh yeah. And what might that be?"

"A gold ring," I said.

The pudgy-faced guy exchanged a quick glance with Chimp. So much for his I'm-not-really-interested act.

"And you handed it over to the Old Bill, did you?" he asked.

"Yeah, course I did," I lied. "It's important evidence, isn't it?"

"Is it?" said Pudgy-Face. He gave a leery smile. "That's what they told you, did they?"

His smug manner was annoying me. I was fed up with his teasy sort of questions.

"Maybe," I said, teasing a bit myself. "That's between us, isn't it?"

He laughed at that. So did Chimp next to him. "So you think you're clever, eh?" said Pudgy-Face. "You'd better watch out you don't trip over your tongue." He nodded at Fish. "What about him there? Don't he speak?"

"Course he does!" I hissed before Fish could reply. "He just doesn't like to waste his words, that's all."

"What's your name, son?" Pudgy-Face demanded.

"Fish," said Fish.

Pudgy-Face laughed again. "That ain't a name," he said. "That's a thing with fins."

Fish shrugged. "It's what I'm called," he said coolly.

Pudgy-Face wagged his head, like he was thinking about this. "Well look here, Fish," he said at last, "me and my pal here happen to have a personal interest in what … happened on the Common. So if you know anything about it, then we'd like to know about it too. Understand?"

Fish nodded.

"You call me at *Bob's Place.* It's a restaurant." He smiled broadly. "A *fish* restaurant." He and Chimp thought that was really funny. They had a right laugh.

I snorted like it was the most pathetic joke I'd heard – which it was pretty much. Pudgy-Face didn't like that. His small, light eyes got nasty. "You want to be careful, girl," he said, waving a beefy finger at me. "You don't want to go messing with guys like us. People who mess with us don't come out well." He dragged his finger across his throat. "Get my meaning?"

This time it was Fish who got in before *me*. "She's just got a big mouth," he said. "She doesn't mean anything."

Pudgy-Face looked at my spiky hair. "Yeah, well, you'd better tell Cockatoo here to put a sock in it," he said. "A big sock." He nodded his head at the driver and the car pulled quickly away. Within seconds, it was round the corner and out of our sight.

Chapter 3
A Good Idea?

I was furious. I was angry about the way those goons had treated me. But I was even more angry with Fish.

"What d'you mean telling those creeps I've got a big mouth. You on their side or something?" I fumed. Then I stormed off.

I wouldn't talk to Fish until we were in our secret place later. I'd calmed down a bit by then. But I was still pretty mad.

"Look, Ros, those guys meant business," Fish said in that oh-so-reasonable way of his. "We're not dealing with school kids. If you start getting all cocky they're likely to break your legs or something. I was trying to stop you getting in trouble."

I snorted, "Huh, I'm not afraid of those goons," I said.

"Well you should be, Ros," Fish said. He gave me a really serious stare. "I am."

Well, that shut me up for a moment. Fish doesn't scare easily. He's used to standing up for himself – well, sitting up for himself anyway. I've seen him face down jokers who thought he was an easy target plenty of times. So when he said he was afraid, it made me think.

"I'm not sure you should have told that lie about giving the police the ring," Fish went on.

14

I shrugged. "They don't know it was a lie, do they?"

"Not yet," said Fish, "but I bet they soon will."

"Yeah, well, maybe," I said. I sat in silence for a minute or two on the big, white stone that was my special seat, gazing down at the gold ring in my hand.

When I looked up, Fish was staring at me. "What are we going to do?" he asked.

"I don't know," I said and I looked down again. The thing was, an idea *had* just come into my head. But I wasn't sure Fish would like it. In fact, I *knew* he wouldn't like it. It was to do with that ring. And it was risky. Really dangerous in fact.

"You're planning something, Ros, aren't you?" Fish said.

I should have known I couldn't hide anything from Fish. Sometimes I think we can read each other's minds!

"I did have a little thought," I said with a sheepish grin. I sighed. "Look, Fish, those goons we met were clearly involved in that bloke's murder, right?"

Fish nodded.

"Well, what if this ring *has* got something to do with it all. Maybe it belongs to one of the gang and could prove they were involved. It's got a 'T' on, that's an important clue, isn't it?"

"Go on," Fish said.

"Well, if it *does* belong to one of them, I bet they'll want it back." I paused, closing my hand around the ring. "I think they'd want it pretty badly."

"Badly enough to pay someone big money for it," Fish added, grasping my meaning.

16

"Exactly," I said. "It would be perfect justice, wouldn't it? Them paying us money to help Darren kick his habit, when it was their drugs that did the damage in the first place."

"But if the ring is evidence," Fish reasoned, "shouldn't we give it to the police to help convict the person that did the murder?"

"You saw how they treated us today, Fish," I said. "They must know who did the crime. I don't think they're bothered. Like the papers said, it's a gangland thing. That's one less hoodlum for them to worry about, isn't it?"

Fish thought about this for a moment or two. "I don't think it's a good idea, Ros," he said at last. "I don't think it's a good idea at all." He looked straight at me, "But you've made your mind up, haven't you?"

I nodded. "I've got to do this – for Darren," I said softly.

Fish sighed. Then he smiled, "Well, we'd better make sure it's a good plan ..."

Chapter 4
Aunt Jenny and Uncle Ted

That evening we went round to Fish's Aunt Jenny's house for supper. It was something we often did – at least once a week.

We both liked Jenny a lot. She and Fish's mum are sisters, but you'd never know it. They are like chalk and cheese. Fish's mum means well, but she's always fussing. Fish can't stand it. He hates being fussed over. Jenny doesn't fuss. She's very laid back. She cares a lot about Fish – you can see that – but she doesn't try to mollycoddle him, like his mum does. Jenny knows Fish can look after himself.

For me, going round to Jenny's was a sort of escape. I didn't really like being at home. There was only me and Dad now and we didn't have much to say to each other. If we did talk, we ended up arguing. We argued about the state of my room, the way I looked, my general attitude ... Dad always seemed to be on my case these days. Why can't he be more like Uncle Ted? I used to ask myself.

Uncle Ted was Aunt Jenny's husband. They hadn't been married long. In fact, they hadn't known each other long. Looks-wise they were an odd couple, but they were very happy. Jenny was slim and gorgeous, with tumbling, blonde hair; Ted was short and a bit tubby with thinning hair, geeky glasses and a really catchy smile. Jenny said it was his smile that won her over.

Uncle Ted was often away when we went round, but he was there that evening. I think he was the one who raised the subject of the murder on the Common.

Jenny shivered. "That was awful," she said. She nodded at Fish and me as she served out the food. "I hope you two are staying well away."

I felt myself go a bit red and maybe Fish did too, because Jenny clearly sensed that we knew something.

"What have you two been up to?" she asked, as she put our plates in front of us. So Fish told her about our visit to the police – though he didn't mention anything about the ring. He said we'd seen someone hanging round the Common near our den and had gone to report it.

"And what did the police say?" asked Ted.

"Nothing," I said. "They weren't interested."

"No, they never are," said Ted, "unless you've got some hard evidence." He smiled. "You didn't have any evidence to show them, did you?"

I glanced at Fish and he glanced back at me. Jenny was watching us.

"There's something you haven't told us, isn't there?" she said. "Come on, out with it."

Fish glanced at me again and I shrugged. "Might as well tell them," I said. Fish nodded.

"We got stopped on the way back home," he said and he told Jenny and Ted about our meeting with the goons.

Jenny was shocked. Her face went really pale. "Did you go back to the police?" she said. We shook our heads. "You should have done," she insisted.

22

Ted put his hand on her arm. "There wouldn't have been any point, love," he said. "They'd already said they weren't interested."

"But it sounds to me as if Fish and Ros could be in danger," Jenny persisted. "The police should do something about it."

Ted smiled. "They're trying to solve a murder," he said.

"Me and Ros can look after ourselves," said Fish with confidence. "Isn't that right, Ros?"

"Yeah," I agreed. "Don't worry about us, Jenny."

But Jenny did look worried. "Just you be careful," she said.

Chapter 5
Tommy Dayton

Next day, I made a phone call to *Bob's Place* to set up a meeting with Pudgy-Face. A car would pick me up, I was told, on the edge of the Common at four o'clock sharp.

"You'd better be there," the voice on the phone warned.

"I'll be there," I said.

I told Fish what I'd done. He wanted to come too. But I told him I was going on my own. He couldn't get his wheelchair into the car anyway, I pointed out.

"I could dial a special taxi and follow you," he said.

But I shook my head. "No," I said. "You've got to look after the ring." I took the gold ring out of my pocket and handed it to him. "Put it somewhere safe," I said. "My life might depend upon it."

He took the ring and zipped it into his jacket pocket. "I wish I was going with you, Ros," he sighed.

"I know," I said. "But it's better this way."

I felt a bit guilty because the real reason I didn't want Fish to come with me was that I didn't want anything to happen to him. The look on Jenny's face had spooked me a bit. What I was about to do was dangerous and I didn't want Fish sharing the danger. This was my fight really, not his.

"Well, at least take my mobile," he said, pressing his phone into my hand. "You might need it."

"Thanks," I said and I slipped it into the inside pocket of my jacket.

The car was late. It was a damp, grey day and I didn't fancy hanging around and catching a cold. I was peeking at my watch for about the tenth time in as many minutes when, at last, the big, white car drew up. The back door swung open, inviting me in. I made a point of looking down at my watch, then ambled over to the car.

Pudgy-Face was waiting for me. Chimp was sitting in the front with the driver. "Don't hurry yourself, will you," Pudgy-Face hissed.

"You're the one who's late, not me," I replied, getting in beside him. I pulled the door shut behind me and the car drove away.

The car smelt strongly of leather and aftershave. It was so strong it made me splutter.

"What's the matter, Cockatoo?" said Pudgy-Face. "Scared?"

"The only thing I'm scared of is being gassed to death by your aftershave," I said.

Pudgy-Face gave a nasty grin. "Yeah, well, it's better than the smell of someone pooing their pants," he said.

"Who's pooing their pants?" I said.

"We'll see, Cockatoo, we'll see," he said with menace.

The car drove through town and on. We were heading towards the old quarry now, where the gravel works used to be. It was a miserable, lonely place at the best of times, but in today's grey drizzle, it looked like a vale of tears. I hoped they wouldn't turn out to be mine. I have to admit I was starting to get a bit nervous. I hadn't planned on this happening.

The car drew to a halt finally on a bit of wasteground above the gravel works. There was a man standing at the edge of the quarry, gazing down. He was wearing a long, dark coat with the collar turned up. I couldn't see his face, because he had his back to us, but I knew this must be the boss. Pudgy-Face and Chimp escorted me to him.

The man must have heard us coming, our shoes crunching across the damp gravel, but he didn't turn. In fact, he didn't move at all. He just kept on looking down. When we were about ten metres away, Pudgy-Face and Chimp stopped. Without turning, the man raised his hand and signalled for me to come closer.

I looked across when I came level with him. He had a thin, sharp face. A deep scar ran from just below his ear to his chin. His dark hair was slicked against his scalp and was shiny from the rain.

"What's your name, kid?" he muttered at last. His voice was hoarse and oddly high in tone. When he spoke, his lips hardly moved at all.

"Ros," I said. "Ros Fowler."

He nodded, as if it was a name he knew well.

"Well, Ros," he said. "Do you know who I am?"

"No," I said truthfully.

He nodded again, still staring ahead. "My name's Tommy Dayton," he said. Then, finally, he turned his face towards me. He had the coldest, hardest eyes I'd ever seen and they were full of darkness. There was something about them that didn't look human. "You may have heard of me," he suggested.

I nodded. Yeah, I'd heard of Tommy Dayton all right. Everyone round our way had heard of Tommy Dayton. He was the Mr Big of the local crime world. Anything bad that went down, you could be pretty sure Tommy Dayton was involved somewhere. And here I was face to face with him, just a few metres of gravel between us.

"So, Ros, I understand you've got something to tell me." He turned away again. "I'm listening ... just."

His voice made my heart thump. I wished Fish was with me. "I found something on the Common the other day, near the scene of that murder," I said, hoping my voice didn't sound as wobbly as it felt in my throat. "A gold ring."

Tommy Dayton nodded. "A ring," he repeated without expression.

"Yes," I said, "with the letter 'T' on it." I paused to let this sink in. But Tommy Dayton

31

didn't react at all. "I thought it might be worth something to someone," I added with a boldness I wasn't feeling.

Tommy Dayton sighed. "I see," he breathed. Then he raised a hand and signalled for Pudgy-Face and Chimp to step forward.

"Yes, boss?" Pudgy-Face inquired.

Tommy Dayton looked down at the dingy gravel works. "Throw her over," he ordered.

It took me a moment or two to take in what he'd said. By then Pudgy-Face and Chimp were on me, each grabbing an arm. They started to drag me backwards towards the edge.

"Hey!" I cried. I struggled, but they were much too strong for me. Their hands on my arm were like iron bands.

"My friend's got the ring!" I shrieked in terror. My feet were already dangling in the air. "If I don't go back, he'll take it to the police!" In another moment, I'd be dropping through the air on to the hard ground far below. I'd be a goner.

Tommy Dayton clicked his fingers. "Stop!" he commanded. "Bring her back." Pudgy-Face and Chimp pulled me back from the edge and pushed me down to the ground. Then they stepped away and made a big show of tidying themselves, as if touching me had made them dirty.

Tommy Dayton walked across and stood over me. "You've got 24 hours, Ros," he said darkly. "If that ring isn't in my hands by the end of tomorrow, well ..." He pointed towards the drop with his finger, "You and your friend will be taking a little trip." His eyes were so hard they could have been made of stone. "And you won't be coming back." With that, he turned and walked over to the car.

Pudgy-Face and Chimp followed him.

It wasn't until they'd driven away that I dared to try and get up. And then I was shaking so much, I had to sit back down again.

Chapter 6
More Threats

I called Fish on his mobile. I was shivering so much I could hardly speak. I'm not sure if it was from the cold and wet or the shock of what I'd just gone through.

"You sound terrible, Ros," Fish said. He asked me where I was and said he'd come out to get me. There's this special dial-a-ride taxi service he can call up because he's in a wheelchair. He hardly ever uses it, but I was certainly glad of it now.

By the time Fish arrived, I'd pulled myself together a bit, but I was chilled to the bone. On the way back to town, I told Fish what had happened.

He was horrified. "I knew you shouldn't have gone on your own, Ros," he said.

I smiled weakly. "Now who's being over-protective?" I said.

Fish had some news of his own. He'd had a call from one of Tommy Dayton's gang – Pudgy-Face, he reckoned. The caller had made the same kind of grim threats that Tommy Dayton had made to me.

"I wonder how he got your phone number," I said.

"They know everything," said Fish gloomily. "They even know about Jenny and Ted."

"What d'you mean?" I asked.

"Well, it wasn't just me they threatened. They said that if they didn't get the ring back then Uncle Ted would be sorry too."

"*Ted*?"

"Yeah," Fish confirmed.

"But why Ted?" I persisted. I couldn't get my head round that.

"I suppose they know how much Jenny and Ted mean to me," said Fish. "Maybe they followed us round to their house yesterday."

"Maybe," I shrugged. "But was it both of them they threatened or just Ted?"

Fish frowned. "Well, now you come to mention it," he said, "I think it was just Ted. I just took it to mean both of them."

"That's weird, don't you think?" I said.

"Yes, I suppose," said Fish uncertainly.

We sat in silence for a moment or so.

"Hasn't Ted got a gold ring?" I asked at last. "I'm sure I've seen him wearing one. But I can't remember if he was wearing it last night."

Fish nodded. "Yes, he has got one," he agreed. "But surely Ros you're not suggesting the ring we found is his? What could Ted have to do with all this?" He paused, then added, "Besides, Ted isn't his real name. It's short for Edward, isn't it? His ring would have an 'E' on it, not a 'T'."

I let out a heavy sigh. "Yeah, you're right," I said. "I just can't think straight at the moment." Suddenly, I started to shiver again as the scariness of that meeting out at the old gravel works caught up with me. I slumped forward against Fish and he put his arms round me.

"Fish, what are we going to do?" I muttered.

Then I started to cry.

38

Chapter 7
Interrogation

When I got home, another nasty surprise was waiting for me.

I saw a police car parked outside our house but didn't take much notice. There was nothing odd about seeing police cars round our way. Only this time it was my house the police were visiting.

Dad didn't look at all happy.

"There are two policemen here to see you, Rosalind," he said, "they seem to think you might know something about that murder on the Common. They say you've been down to talk to them already."

"Yeah, I went with Fish," I said, as if this explained everything. To be honest, I just wanted a bath and to get into bed. The last thing I wanted was to face a grilling from Dad and the police. But there was no getting out of it.

It was the same two policemen that had talked – or *not* talked – to Fish and me down at the police station. Only now they were all friendly and attentive. I smelt a rat.

"We think you may have something of interest to us," said Inspector Morris, the senior policeman. "Some important evidence regarding the murder last week."

I stared at them blankly. "What's that then?" I said.

"A ring," said Inspector Morris. "We believe it was lost at the time of the incident. We think it could be a vital piece of evidence."

My mouth fell open. It seemed like everyone knew everything about me and Fish and the ring. It was like the whole of our lives were on camera or something.

"Who told you about this ring?" I asked.

Inspector Morris smiled. "We have our sources, Ros," he said with a knowing smile.

I hadn't liked him at the police station and I liked him even less now. He was smug like Pudgy-Face. He thought he was in total control.

"Well, your sources got it wrong," I said. "I don't know anything about a ring."

The smile fell away. "Don't mess about, Ros," he said and he gave me what he probably thought was a hard, steely stare. "We know you've got that ring – and we need

41

it. It's our belief that it belongs to Tommy Dayton." He paused, as if waiting for me to react – which I didn't. "We've been after Tommy Dayton for a long time," he went on, "and with that ring, we think we could nail him. He's a nasty piece of work, Tommy Dayton, and it's about time he got what was coming to him."

"I'm sorry," I said. "I'd help if I could – honest I would. But I can't."

Inspector Morris gave up on me and turned his attention to Dad. "Mr Fowler," he said, "your daughter could be in serious trouble unless she co-operates with us. Withholding evidence is a very serious offence."

I expected Dad to take the policemens' side and start bugging me, but he didn't. In fact, he amazed me by doing the opposite.

"I don't like your tone, Officer," he said. "My daughter has told you what she knows and now I'd like you to leave." And that was that. They went.

"You're playing a dangerous game, Ros," Inspector Morris warned me as he left. Yeah, I thought, tell me about it.

"Ros, you'd better be telling the truth about this," Dad said sternly when he had closed the front door.

It seemed like I was getting one threat after another these days.

Chapter 8
A Difficult Choice

Fish and I didn't go to school the next morning. We went down to our secret place on the Common instead to have a think. This was the most important day of our lives. If we weren't careful, it could be the *last* day of our lives too.

I brought Fish up-to-date with the police visit.

"So it's Tommy Dayton's ring," Fish said.

"It seems like it," I agreed.

"That's good," Fish said.

I could tell there was something on his mind. "Why's it good?" I said.

"Well, 'cos it means it's not Ted's," Fish said. He wriggled a bit in his chair. "I found out last night that Ted's not short for Edward. His real name's Theodore."

"*Theodore*!" I exclaimed.

"Yeah," said Fish and we both laughed. "Jenny says there was a famous American President called Theodore Roosevelt. He was called Teddy for short and that's where the name teddy bear comes from."

"What, the President of the United States was a teddy bear?" I joked. "Don't tell me his wife was called Barbie."

"No, of course not," Fish scoffed. We were both laughing now. We laughed loud and long. It felt good.

"You know what?" I said when we'd calmed down. "That's the first time I've laughed in days."

"Yeah, me too," said Fish.

"You have got the ring safe, haven't you?" I said.

Fish nodded. Then he took it out of his jacket pocket. He held it on his palm.

"What are we going to do with it?" he asked.

"Give it up, I suppose," I said.

"Yeah, but who to?" Fish said.

I kicked my heel against the white stone I was sitting on. "I don't know," I said.

It was one hell of a decision. If we gave the ring to the police, we were dead; if we gave it to Tommy Dayton, he would be getting away with murder. But there was something else nagging at me too. Uncle Ted – Theodore.

What if he was mixed up in it all somehow, however unlikely that was? Well, maybe what we did would affect him too. And that meant Jenny being affected ...

I told these concerns to Fish.

"But you said the ring was Tommy Dayton's," Fish argued.

"I said that's what the police believe," I said. "But what if it did belong to Ted? Maybe Tommy Dayton's trying to frame him or something."

"But then he'd want us to give the ring to the police, wouldn't he?" Fish reasoned.

"Unless he wanted the ring so that he'd have a hold over him," I said.

"Don't complicate things, Ros." Fish sounded weary. "Either we give the ring to Tommy Dayton or we give it to the police. Ted's not involved." He gazed at the gold ring in his palm. Then he closed his hand and looked up at me. "Look," he said suddenly, "Ted went away last night to Paris. He's flying back this afternoon and Jenny's going to meet him at the airport. She asked me if I wanted to go to keep her company. Why don't you come too? If Ted's wearing his ring, you'll know for sure he's not involved. Then whatever we decide to do, it'll only affect us."

I shook my head and gave Fish a frowny smile. "Is that supposed to make me feel better?" I said.

"It's best to know the truth," said Fish.

And he spoke with such feeling that I dared not contradict him.

Chapter 9
Waiting

Ted's plane from Paris was delayed for an hour due to bad weather. We waited for him in one of the lounges overlooking the runway and Jenny treated us to hot chocolate and Danish pastries.

"You two are very quiet today," she remarked. "Is something worrying you?"

"It's just exams," Fish lied. "We've got a lot of work to do."

"You should have told me," Jenny said, "I wouldn't have asked you to come with me if I'd known."

"We wanted to come," I said smiling. "We need the break."

"Oh, OK," said Jenny. She sighed. "I think *I* could do with a break. Ted's been so busy lately. I hardly see him – except at the airport. We're like passing planes." She smiled sort of sadly. Then she touched my arm. "How's your Dad doing, Ros? I've always really admired the way he gets on with things. It must have been so hard for him with all that's happened over the last few years. Well, it must have been hard for all of you."

"Yeah, I suppose so," I muttered.

"And how's Darren?" Jenny continued. "He's coming home soon, isn't he?"

"Yes," I said. I'd been so busy over the

past days that I'd forgotten about Darren coming home. Well, now it didn't look like I'd be there to greet him. In fact, I thought with a shudder, I didn't know whether I'd ever see him again.

"Are you OK, Ros?" said Jenny. "You've gone very pale."

"Yes," I said. "I'm fine."

"She still gets upset about what happened to Darren," Fish explained.

"Yes, of course," said Jenny and *she* looked really upset. "I think those drug dealers are really evil. But the police don't seem to be able to do anything about them, do they?"

"No," I said quietly. I thought briefly about the ring zipped-up in Fish's jacket.

"It's that Tommy Dayton," Jenny insisted. "He's the one they want to get. We'd all sleep better if he was locked away."

Fish and I glanced at one another guiltily. I was just about to say something, when Ted's flight flashed up on the arrivals screen. It had just touched down, half an hour late.

"Time to go," said Jenny.

We waited at the exit for Ted to appear. Stranger after stranger flowed past, some with loaded trolleys, some with nothing but a briefcase. I was feeling really on edge now. *What*, I wondered, *if Ted wasn't wearing his ring? What would that prove? What difference would it make?*

Fish looked really edgy too. He kept tapping his hands against the armrests of his wheelchair, which I knew was a sure sign that he was feeling tense.

At last, Ted appeared, wheeling a black suitcase. About 20 metres away he spotted us and paused for a moment. He raised his hand and waved.

Even at that distance I could clearly see the chunky gold ring on his little finger. Fish and I looked at each other and smiled. The ring we had wasn't his.

Chapter 10
Decision Time

On the way home from the airport, Fish and I told Jenny and Ted about the ring and the police and my meeting with Tommy Dayton. It was an amazing relief. At last, we'd revealed the truth – well, most of it. We didn't say anything about suspecting Ted might be involved. I think we both felt too ashamed.

Jenny was horrified. She wanted to take us down to the police station right away.

"You need protection," she said. "You've got to go."

Neither Fish nor I felt convinced that the police would protect us – especially after what that policeman had said on leaving my house. He'd seemed to suggest that *we* were criminals.

Ted was concerned, but a bit calmer than Jenny. He asked us what *we* wanted to do.

"I dunno," I shrugged. "I just want it to be all over."

"Yeah," Fish agreed. "I wish we'd never found the stupid ring."

"But you did," Ted pointed out, "and Tommy Dayton knows it." The mention of Tommy Dayton made me shudder, recalling those dark, inhuman eyes. "So either you give him back the ring and walk away," Ted continued, "or you give the ring to the police. There's nothing else you can do, is there?"

"No," I muttered. We were back to the same old problem. Neither choice seemed right.

"You have to go to the police," Jenny insisted.

It was all right for *her*, I thought bitterly.

"What do you think, Ted?" Fish asked.

Ted pushed his glasses up on the bridge of his nose. Behind them, his eyes were strangely serious. "I wouldn't want to force you to do anything," he said, "it's your decision. But if you really want to know what I think, well, I agree with Jenny. Tommy Dayton is a nasty piece of work. He's ruined a lot of innocent lives." He nodded at me. "Look at your Darren, for example. I think it's time he was made to pay for his crimes." He frowned. "But, like I say, it's *your* decision."

"Yeah, thanks for reminding us," I said with a sarcastic smile.

"We'll support you all the way," Jenny told us. "You won't be on your own."

"That's right," Ted nodded, smiling, "I'll protect you."

That really made me smile. Somehow the idea of tubby, friendly Uncle Ted protecting me against Tommy Dayton, Pudgy-Face, Chimp and the rest wasn't much comfort. It was a generous offer though and I was grateful for it.

"Thanks," I said.

"Yeah," Fish added.

We looked at one another. "Looks like we're off to the police, then," I said.

"Looks like it," Fish agreed.

Jenny was all for taking us down to the police station right there and then. Ted too. But I didn't want to. I don't know why exactly – maybe it was just my stubborn nature. I wanted a bit of time on my own to think things through. I knew what I had to do, but I didn't feel quite prepared yet to do it. I told the others I wanted to talk to my dad. And I did. I really did. But I was playing for time too.

We were back in town now. I looked out at the gloomy evening air smudged with yellow from the streetlights. "We'll go to the police first thing in the morning," I promised.

Chapter 11
Running Away

Ted and Jenny dropped me and Fish off at his house. I lifted his wheelchair out of the boot and set it up and helped him get settled. Then I asked him for the ring.

"Why?" he asked.

"Tommy Dayton knows you've got it. It'll be safer with me," I explained.

He handed it over with reluctance.

"I'll give you a call later," I said. I remembered I still had his mobile and I took it out of my pocket to give it back. But he shook his head.

"You hold on to it, Ros," he said.

"Why?" I said.

He shrugged. "I don't know," he said. "I just want you to." He gave me a half smile. "I won't worry about you so much."

I shook my head, grinning. "You don't have to worry about me," I said.

"But I do," he replied and he gave me this look like he could see right into me. "Just be careful, all right?" he said.

"Yeah, yeah," I said. But I put the phone back in my pocket anyway, just to keep him happy. "We'll talk later, OK?" I said airily. Then I set off on the short walk home.

I was deep in thought as I turned the corner into my street. That was why I didn't see the car straight away. I was almost on it before the message got from my eyes to my brain that there was a big, white car outside my house and that Pudgy-Face and his mates were sitting in it, waiting for me. But as soon as I realised, I didn't hesitate. I turned and ran.

There were shouts behind me, so I knew they'd seen me. I heard the car start up and the screech of tyres as it turned to follow me. I was round the corner, but in moments they would be too and the street stretched out straight and empty ahead of me. They'd catch me long before I reached the end of it.

The blood was pounding in my ears. I had to think of something fast.

As the car rounded the corner, I dived over a low wall and into a bushy front garden. I rolled close to the wall, hoping that I couldn't be seen from the street. The car

sped by. But I knew it would be back. I'd
gained myself a couple of minutes that was
all.

In an instant I was on my feet again. I ran
down the side of the house and into the back
garden. This was even more overgrown than
the front. I could hear the car coming back
slowly down the street. I struggled through
the jungle of weeds and brambles towards the
fence at the end of the garden.

I'd got about halfway, when a fox suddenly
shot out of the bushes and skulked off into
the garden next door. I'm not usually a nervy
person, but at that moment I nearly jumped
out of my skin. I cried out too – and then
cursed, as I heard a shout in the street
behind me. Now Pudgy-Face and his crew
knew where I was.

I still had a lead on them, though, and I
had one big advantage – I knew the area. In

seconds I'd reached the fence and was over, dropping into the garden beyond.

I sprinted across the well-cut lawn, not caring who saw me. Then I was down the side alley and out through the gate.

Now I felt safe. For a while at least. In front of me lay the perfect hiding place – huge, dense, dark: the Common.

Chapter 12
Time's Up

I sat on my white seat in our secret place, staring at the ring in my hand. Something was bugging me. Something wasn't right – apart from the fact that I was likely to end up dead the way things were going.

It was a funny thing, though, I wasn't that worried about dying. I mean I didn't have a death wish or anything, but with all the things that had happened in the last few years – losing Mum and then very nearly losing Darren too – well, death didn't really freak me that much.

I took out Fish's mobile and dialled the number for *Bob's Place*.

"Bob's not here," a gruff voice said.

"Well, I need to talk to him," I said. "My name's Ros Fowler."

"Oh," said the voice. "Bob's been looking for you."

"I know," I said. I gave him Fish's mobile number. "Tell him, if he wants the ring, he'd better call me – quickly."

"I'll tell him," said the man.

Within a minute of the call ending, Fish's phone started to beep.

"Yeah?" I said.

"Well, Cockatoo," said Pudgy-Face. "Time's up."

"I've got the ring," I said.

"Of course you have," said Pudgy-Face, "and now you're going to hand it over. Where are you?"

I snorted. "You think I'm that stupid?" I said. "If I tell you where I am, you'll come over, take the ring and get rid of me while you're at it. I don't think so."

Pudgy-Face sighed. "You're putting ideas in my head, Cockatoo," he said, trying to stay cool. "You don't want to do that."

"Well, there's nothing *else* in there," I sneered.

This time he made no attempt to act cool. "Just give me the ring, Cockatoo," he hissed, "or you'll be sorry. Very sorry."

Suddenly, I knew what was wrong, what had been bugging me. "How come the police know I've got the ring?" I said. "I only told you and Tommy Dayton and that chimp that hangs around with you. Are you double-dealing, or something? Fancy taking over Tommy's place, do you?"

"What are you talking about?"

"Someone told the police about the ring. They came round to my house asking about it. So who's been talking? It's certainly not me."

"Well it ain't me, Cockatoo. And it ain't Harry neither." Harry must be Chimp, I reckoned.

"Well, I don't trust either of you," I said. A new idea was forming in my head. "I'll give the ring to Tommy Dayton and no-one else. Tell him to meet me by the old air-raid shelter on the Common at nine o'clock sharp. I'll be watching. If he brings anyone else along, the ring goes to the police."

Chapter 13
More Calls

My next call was to the police. I asked to speak to Inspector Morris. I wrapped my T-shirt round the phone to muffle my voice and spoke as low as I could. I probably sounded ridiculous, but right then I didn't give a monkey's.

I told Inspector Morris where he would find the ring.

"If you want it, you'd better get there fast," I said. "Tommy Dayton's going to be there in exactly 26 minutes."

"Who's this speaking?" he said.

I rang off. Then I wiped the ring to clean off any fingerprints I might have left and scuffed it in the earth for good measure. Using my T-shirt as a kind of glove, I put the ring carefully back where Fish and I had discovered it a couple of days before.

I rang home. The answerphone was on, so I left a message.

"Dad, things are bad. I'm going to have to go away for a while," I said. "I can't explain it all to you now, but Jenny and Ted know about it. Say 'hi' to Darren for me, will you? I'm sorry I won't be there to welcome him. I'll call you again soon." I had to bite my lip to stop myself from crying. "Don't worry about me, Dad. I love you. See you. Bye."

I breathed deeply and tried to calm myself, before calling Jenny and Ted. The line was engaged. I called Fish.

"Ros," he said, his voice breathless with concern, "where are you? Your dad's been round here with Jenny looking for you. They're really worried."

"I'm in our den," I said, "on the Common." I told him about everything that had gone on since I'd left him.

"You'd better get out of there," Fish said. "You don't want to be there when Tommy Dayton arrives."

"I'm leaving now," I said. "Fish, I reckon I'll have to clear off for a while, until things cool down a bit."

"I'll come with you," Fish said, as I knew he would.

"No, you can't," I said.

"You can't go off on your own," Fish insisted.

I took another deep breath before going on, "Fish, you're paralysed. You're in a wheelchair. There's no way you can come with me. It's just not possible." Fish said nothing.

I felt terrible. I'd always been so supportive of Fish and now I'd said just about the meanest thing I possibly could. But I couldn't let Fish come with me. It just wouldn't have been right. I cared too much about him. "I'm going round to Jenny and Ted's now," I said. "Those threats Tommy Dayton's gang made against Ted, well, he could be in danger. I need to warn him. I tried phoning but the line was busy." I was gabbling now, I knew. "Say something, Fish," I pleaded. "Wish me luck or something. Call me a cow if you like. But don't go silent on me."

"Good luck," Fish said dully. I'd really hurt him, I could tell.

"I'll leave your phone round at Jenny's," I said. "See you."

"See you," said Fish. Then a split second later he added in an urgent tone, "Ros, if you need anything, call me."

"Yeah," I said. "Thanks. Thanks a lot, Fish."

I rang off and ran out into the dark, hoping there was no-one close enough to hear my sobs.

Chapter 14
A Price to Pay

I was worried that I was too late. As I got near Jenny's house, Chimp came out. Luckily he wasn't looking my way. I jumped behind a fence, my heart thumping. Glancing out, I saw Chimp get into a car and drive away.

I sprinted down the road, praying that nothing terrible had happened to Uncle Ted. How would I ever forgive myself for not warning him?

I rang the bell several times. With each ring, my heart grew more and more heavy. When the door finally opened, I was slumped against the wall.

"Ros?" Ted looked out at me from behind the half-opened door, frowning with surprise.

"Ted," I breathed. I sighed deeply with relief. "I thought something had happened to you," I said.

"No, I'm fine," he said, still frowning. "But you look awful. You'd better come in." I followed Ted through to the sitting room and collapsed into an armchair.

"Jenny's not here at the moment," Ted said.

"I know," I said. "I think she's with my dad, looking for me. I'm running away."

Ted stood over me. He looked uneasy. But then, I supposed, it wasn't every day that a tired and tearful teenage girl turned up on his doorstep. "Let me get you a drink or something," he offered.

"No, it's OK," I said. Then I told him why I'd come and what I was doing. "When I saw that goon come out of here just now," I said, "I was really scared they'd done something to you. And then, when you didn't answer the door ..."

"I was on the phone," Ted said quickly. He looked even more uneasy now. I'd never seen his face look so serious. There was clearly something worrying him.

Something new was worrying me too. "What was that goon doing here?" I said.

Ted pushed his glasses up on his nose and took a deep breath. "Ros," he said at last, "I've been a bit of a fool. In fact, I've been a complete idiot. I've got myself mixed up in things that, well," he shook his head wearily, "I shouldn't have done."

"What sort of things?" I asked.

"Bad things," he said, and then Ted told me.

About six months before, Ted's business was in trouble. A deal went wrong and he lost a lot of money. He needed to get some more fast or he'd lose everything – not only his business, but his house, car, maybe even Jenny, he thought. They hadn't known each other for that long then.

He went to the bank and a few other places, but no-one would help him out – he was too much of a risk. So, in desperation, he went to a loan shark and that brought him into contact with Tommy Dayton. Money lending, drugs, protection rackets, they were all controlled by Tommy Dayton. Well, he agreed to lend Ted money, but at a price. Ted had expected that. He knew he'd have to pay a high price, but hadn't been ready for what Tommy Dayton demanded. He wanted to use

Ted's business to launder his dirty money – the profits of his crimes – so that it couldn't be traced back to him. It was one thing to borrow dirty money from a criminal, but quite another to launder it. That was crossing the line into crime.

"I should never have done it," Ted concluded. "But I was desperate. I could see no other option." He sighed. "I've regretted it bitterly ever since."

"So that's what they meant about harming you," I said, thinking out loud. "If we didn't hand back the ring, they'd expose you. It was blackmail."

"I guess you could say that," Ted agreed.

A nasty thought struck me. "But if the police get the ring and arrest Tommy Dayton, won't you be in trouble too?"

"I suppose so," Ted nodded.

"But you told us to take the ring to the police."

"It's the price I'd have to pay," Ted said. "Like I said last night, it's time that Tommy Dayton was put away."

I admired Ted for taking a stand, but it made me feel terrible. If my set-up had worked, then at that very moment, Tommy Dayton was being captured, ring in hand, by Inspector Morris and his crew. I told Ted what I'd done.

His face relaxed a little. There was the hint of a smile. "You did right, Ros," he said.

The phone started to ring in another room. "I'd better get that," Ted said. He got up and walked out into the hall.

Chapter 15
The Truth

I felt really bad. My plan had seemed so perfect. No-one would be affected but me, I'd thought. I could run away and everyone would be OK. And now, I discovered, that wasn't so: my plan was going to put Ted in deep water. He'd be ruined, go to prison probably. Jenny would be heartbroken.

Everything was so complicated. The strain of it all was really getting to me. I should have felt proud and pleased at what I'd done, but I just felt weary and flat. I wanted to lie down and close my eyes – and the sofa looked very inviting. I went over and slumped on to it. Now all I needed was a cushion for my head ... I grabbed one that looked nice and soft from the end of the sofa by my feet. In doing so I uncovered a bulky brown envelope.

I stared at it for moment or two. A tired voice in my head said, *lie down, get some rest while you can, it's just an envelope.* But another voice said, *pick it up, take a look, if it's just any old envelope, why was it hidden under a cushion?* The second voice won out. I leant forward and picked up the envelope. I hadn't expected it to be so heavy. I soon found out why. It was filled with small, clear plastic bags packed with white powder. I knew what the powder was and what it could do to people. Well, it had almost killed my brother, hadn't it?

I was holding one of the bags of scag when Ted came back in. He looked at me then looked at the bag in my hand.

"So now you know," he said with an easy smile. It was like I'd just found a porno mag rather than a stash of hard drugs.

"Yes," I said. "You're in the gang, aren't you? That goon that was here, he was probably delivering this envelope, wasn't he? And there I was thinking he'd come to do you in." I shook my head with a bitter smile at the madness of it all.

"Harry has his uses," said Ted lightly.

"Like pushing drugs to school kids, you mean," I sneered.

Ted sighed. "That was nothing to do with me, Ros," he said. "Harry thought of that all on his own." He gave a half laugh. "He's not a great thinker, Harry."

"And what about that dead man on the Common?" I demanded. "Did Harry do that too?"

Ted shook his head. "No, that was Tommy. He found out that the guy was informing, you see, and that made him really mad. He just lost it. He beat him up and then killed him. Like a mad dog he was. Tommy's ring must have come off in the struggle."

"And you saw it as your great chance to get rid of Tommy and take over," I sneered. "Funny, I was accusing your mate Pudgy-Face of doing just that earlier today – and all the time it was you. You told the police about the ring, didn't you?"

"Harry told me, after your meeting with Tommy," Ted said. "I just passed on the information," his smile grew broader, "I was just doing my duty, like any good man should."

"Huh," I snorted. "The only thing you're good for is jail."

Ted laughed. "I'm not going to jail," he said. "Tommy Dayton can squawk all he likes, but he's got nothing on me. I covered my tracks. I'm top dog now." The smile that had always seemed so catching and attractive now seemed horribly sinister. Ted's gaze was full on me, his glasses glinting in the overhead light. "The only problem, Ros, is you," he said coolly. "And that's not really a problem any more, is it?"

"Isn't it?" I said.

"No," said Ted. "You said yourself you'd run away. Well, it's amazing how many runaways are never found. Ever."

I didn't like the way this conversation was going one bit. Supposing that phone call was from Harry or some other goon? They could be on their way here at that very instant. It was one thing getting away from tubby Uncle Ted, but I didn't fancy my chances against Harry and any mates he brought with him. I had to get out fast.

Ted saw me glance towards the door. "You can't escape, Ros," he said. He held up a key. "The front door's locked. You can't get out." He was still smiling that unnerving smile.

He took a step towards me and, as he did so, I hurled the bag that I was holding at him. It hit him full in the face, knocking off his glasses. While he bent down to pick them up, I rushed for the door.

Chapter 16
Hide and Seek

I gave a quick tug at the front door. It was locked all right. I could hear Ted crossing the room behind me, so I turned and ran up the stairs.

I stood a moment on the dark landing considering which room to go into. I didn't want to get myself trapped – well, no more trapped than I was already.

"You can't get away, Ros." Ted called from down below. "There's no escape." I heard his footstep on the stairs, coming up slowly. I ran down the passage and into the end room. It was Jenny and Ted's bedroom.

I went over quickly to the windows. It was a fair jump but I'd have risked it, if I could have got the windows open. But they were locked and there was no sign of a key.

"Damn," I cursed. I looked round for somewhere to hide.

"Coming, Ros, ready or not," Ted called again, this time with a chuckle that made my spine tingle. The footsteps were getting closer. I slipped into the wardrobe, pulling the door shut behind me.

I crouched at the back of the wardrobe and pulled a big winter coat down around me. Then I looked around for something that I could use to defend myself. Ted was shortish and tubby, but he was still a grown man, and I was no Gladiator.

My hand felt in the darkness and came across a high-heeled shoe. It wasn't much of a weapon, but it was better than nothing at all. I grasped it tight, holding it up so that the stiletto heel was facing away from me. Then I waited.

The footsteps had stopped now – or at least I couldn't hear them. I crouched in the black listening to the sound of silence. It's amazing just how noisy that sound can be. There was a high-pitched whine in my ears and my heart was beating so hard I felt as if I could hear it.

There was a click like a light switch being turned on. Then a creak as Ted stepped on a loose floorboard. I grasped the high-heeled shoe really tightly. My hand was shaking.

BLEEP!

The sudden noise made me start. I just managed to stop myself crying out. Whatever was making the noise was in the wardrobe with me!

BLEEP!

And then I realised – it was Fish's mobile phone. I put down the shoe and took the phone out of my pocket. *Battery low* was spelt out on the display face. My mind started racing. How low was low? Maybe there'd be enough power for me to phone Fish ...

I'd only pressed out a couple of numbers, when the wardrobe door swung open. I dropped the phone and threw the big winter coat at Ted as he reached in to grab me. As he struggled to free himself from the coat, I dived out of the wardrobe onto the bedroom floor. In a flash I was on my feet and running once more. Seconds later, I was out of the bedroom and crossing the landing. Then I was at the top of the stairs – and disaster struck.

In my haste to get away, I slipped and lost my footing. I tumbled heavily down the stairs.

Everything hurt. I'd banged my head and, from the feel of it, just about every other part of my body as well. I tried to move, but it was just too painful. I was stuck ... and Ted was coming down the stairs towards me.

"I told you there was no escape, Ros," he said – and his voice seemed to come through a haze of cotton wool. "You could have made it easier on yourself, you know."

He was at the bottom of the stairs now. He leant over me, arms outstretched. *This is it*, I thought, *he's going to strangle me*. His hands reached out for my throat ... but before they could settle there was a rattle and a rush of cold air as the front door flew open. Then I was staring upside down at Dad, and watching as his fist lashed out at Ted. Then the hands round my neck dropped away and

Dad's arms were round me instead, holding me, hugging me.

"Ros," he breathed. "Oh, Ros."

Now Jenny's face was there beside Dad's. She was crying.

I closed my eyes. I heard Fish's anxious voice asking, "Is she all right?"

And then there really was silence.

Chapter 17
Reunion

"It's lucky you phoned me and told me where you were going," Fish said. He was sitting in his chair by the side of my hospital bed. Jenny had come in with him. She'd gone off to get some hot chocolate for us all from the vending machine.

"Yeah," I agreed. I moved slightly to get a better view of Fish and groaned as my cracked ribs objected.

"You OK?" Fish asked.

"Yeah," I sighed. "I'll live." Apart from the cracked ribs, I had a broken collarbone, a sprained ankle, a very sore head and about a million bruises. But, like I said, I was alive. "Tell me what happened."

"After you phoned me, Jenny came back," Fish said. "She was so worried about you that I told her about you going round to see Ted. I thought it would make her feel better, but it had the opposite effect. She'd overheard Ted talking on the phone earlier and she was pretty sure he was into something bad. She phoned your dad and we all rushed round." He smiled. "The rest, as they say, is history."

"Yeah, well, thanks," I said. "If you hadn't said anything to Jenny, *I'd* be history." I shivered, recalling Ted's hands tightening around my throat. "I'm really sorry, Fish, about what I said on the phone. I was out of order. It's just that, well ..."

"You wanted to protect me," Fish interrupted. He smiled and shook his head. "I thought you of all people knew, Ros, I can look after myself."

"Yeah, I know," I said.

Jenny arrived with the hot chocolate. "How are you feeling, Ros?" she asked.

"Not too bad, considering," I said.

There were dark circles under Jenny's eyes and her blonde hair was a mess, but she still looked lovely.

"I feel really bad about Ted," she said sadly. "He really took me in."

"He took all of us in," I said thinking, with another shiver, of that grin.

"Well, the police have got him now," Jenny said, "and Tommy Dayton. They caught him over on the Common where that man was murdered. He had enough evidence on him to be sure of a conviction." She gave me a half smile. "They had an anonymous phone call."

I said nothing.

"The papers are full of the arrests," Fish said. "One of them wants to run our story. They're offering a lot of money." He told me how much and I whistled – or tried to. It hurt even to move my lips. But my mind was working all right. With that amount of money we could all go away on a good holiday – me and Darren and Dad – Fish and Jenny too. It seemed only right that they should come. I smiled.

"Hello, Ros." I turned my head to see Dad with a big bunch of roses. They were bright pink to match my hair – what you could see of it beneath the bandages. He leant forward and kissed me on the cheek. His chin was bristly against my skin, but I didn't care. It seemed like a long time since we'd been that close.

And then I saw Darren. He was standing behind Dad, with a shy smile.

"Hi, chump," I said.

He shuffled over and punched me gently on the cheek. "I thought I was the patient," he joked. He looked very pale and thin, but a hell of a lot more like my brother than when I'd last seen him.

"Yeah, well, I thought it was about time I got some attention," I grinned.

I looked round with sudden happiness at the four people standing there, the four people I loved most in the world, gathered about my bed in a ring – a ring of love, a ring of strength, a ring of truth.

Barrington Stoke would like to thank all its readers for commenting on the manuscript before publication and in particular:

Shazrin Akthar
Tom Barge
Ravinder Kaur Bhangle
Sue Black
Helen Coleman
Mandy Collister
Paul Derighetti
Sophie Evans
Michael Fay
Jennie Fulton
Paul Gardner
Edward Healey
Christopher Japp
David Jones
Melissa Lord
Caroline Loven

Andrew Lynes
Dominique MacNeill
Jacqueline Meikle
Caroline Morris
Victoria Nixon
Karen Patterson
Stacy Raiker
Victoria Robson
Mark Sayers
Barbara Sharp
Evelyn Smith
Deborah Walker
Adeline White
Amanda Whitfield
Carla Williams

Become a Consultant!

Would you like to give us feedback on our titles before they are published? Contact us at the address below – we'd love to hear from you!

Barrington Stoke, Sandeman House, Trunk's Close,
55 High Street, Edinburgh EH1 1SR
Tel: 0131 557 2020 Fax: 0131 557 6060
E-mail: info@barringtonstoke.co.uk
Website: www.barringtonstoke.co.uk

If you loved this book, why
don't you read ...

Dream On

by Bali Rai

ISBN 1-842991-95-7

"If you dream, it must be for real ..."

Baljit's mates knew what was
what. If you were good at football,
really good, you could go places.
But all his old man ever talked about
was duty to the family and paying
bills. Baljit couldn't just go on
working in his old man's chippie.
He wanted out!

You can order *Dream On* directly from our
website at **www.barringtonstoke.co.uk**